I Want to Be a Singer and a Veterinarian

Story by

Garrett Carter

Background story
In the world of children's books, there is underrepresentation of African American characters featured as protagonists. This is why I am here—I want to do my part in chipping away at this void. It is important for children to read stories with characters who are similar to and different than them. Introducing Lainey and Coby to the world will allow children of color to see themselves and their culture reflected as they read. Additionally, other children will see that someone who does not look like them might still share many of their thoughts, talents, and dreams.

I also firmly believe that children should not limit themselves to one particular dream. What happens if that singing or athletic career does not work out? Too many children I speak with have not considered this question seriously. I am not discouraging children from dreaming of becoming the next superstar singer or athlete. I am simply encouraging children to have additional dreams. For this reason, I proudly present "Lainey's Singer and Career Series" and "Coby's Athlete and Career Series!"

-Garrett

I Want to Be a Singer and a Veterinarian (Lainey's Singer and Career Series, Book 2)
Summary: Lainey is a young African American girl who is passionate about singing. Lainey discovers that, in addition to being a singer, she could make a great veterinarian!
Text Copyright © 2015 Garrett Carter
Illustrations and Cover art © 2015 Garrett Carter
Illustrated by Anahit Aleksanyan
Edited by Lisa Beckelhimer
Contributions by Nathan Dicke, DVM

ISBN-13: 978-1505705713

Visit the author online: garrettcarterbooks.com and facebook.com/garrettcarterbooks

Daddy, I want to be a singer when I grow up!

I sing as soon as I wake up, all throughout the day, and before I go to bed.

I even *dream* about being a singer!

That's great, Lainey. It's important to have dreams in life. That's *dreams* with the letter *s* on the end. You should dream to be many things.

But singing is what I'm good at, Daddy. I don't know what else I could be besides a singer.

Baby girl, you have many other gifts and talents. Do you remember how you were the first person in our family to notice when Legend got sick? You also helped him get better!

Yes, Daddy! I was so worried about him!

First, I noticed that Legend kept shaking his head a lot.

Next, I saw that he kept scratching at his ears.

I even smelled an odor coming from his ears.

That's when I told you and mom that we needed to take Legend to see the animal doctor…the vet – er…How do you say that word?

Vet – er – i – nar – i – an.

Right! So, Mom called Dr. McKenzie to schedule an appointment.

Once we got to Dr. McKenzie's office, I told her everything I noticed about Legend.

Dr. McKenzie looked in Legend's ears and noticed they were red and swollen; Legend had an ear infection.

I asked her if they are kind of like the ones that people get and she said yes.

She said that Legend needed ear drops twice a day for two weeks and then to bring him back for a checkup.

You did such a great job taking care of Legend.

I sure did, Daddy! Every morning before school I gave Legend his ear drops. I did it again when I got home from school.

After about a week, Legend started to feel better and his ears started to look normal. I had to keep giving him ear drops though until we went back to see Dr. McKenzie.

At Legend's next appointment, Dr. McKenzie said Legend was all better and that I did an excellent job helping him get well. I'm really glad that I was able to help Legend!

Sounds to me like you found something else you might be good at.

I think I want to be a singer *and* a veterinarian!

Remember, baby girl, always have more than one dream.

Looks like Legend has a dream too...

The End

 Hitting the right note!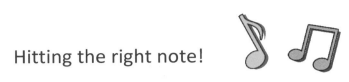

Name: _____

Age: _____ Grade: _____ Today's Date: _____

What hobbies and activities do you enjoy?

_____   _____

_____   _____

List three jobs you might like to have when you are older and explain why they interest you.

1. _____

Why? _____

_____

2. _____

Why? _____

_____

3. _____

Why? _____

_____

What are you doing now to prepare for your future? _____

_____